Don't Look In This Book
ISBN: 978-1-9997628-1-0

First published in the UK
February 2018 by Owlet Press
www.owletpress.com

Text copyright © Samuel Langley-Swain 2018
Illustrations copyright 2019:
© Amberin Huq   @ Christine Cuddihy
© Josh Whitehouse   © Kevin Payne
@ Jemma Banks   © Jessica Martinello
© Francesca Hooper   © Sam Langley-Swain
@ Michaela Hayes

DON'T LOOK IN THIS BOOK!

BY SAMUEL LANGLEY-SWAIN

First published in the UK
February 2018 by Owlet Press
www.owletpress.com

I was talking to you, yes, you right there.

You'd better not look inside.

Don't read on . . . don't you dare!

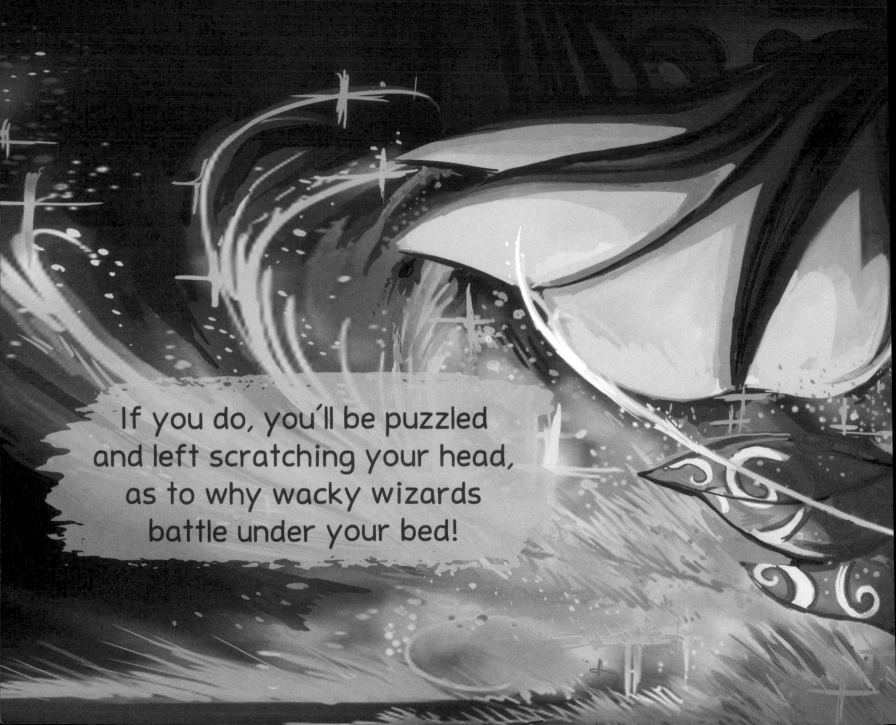

If you do, you'll be puzzled
and left scratching your head,
as to why wacky wizards
battle under your bed!

You'll stumble across the story
of the superhero race,
to see who'd fly their dino-rocket
the fastest into space.

You'll be standing among soldiers
at the bottom of the ocean,
to guard a special shipwreck
that contains a magic potion.

You'll be amazed by aliens flying down from the skies, saving cities from a unicorn with laser beam eyes!

You'll untangle how tigers turned up on a train.
Travelling in tunnels, driving everyone insane!

You'll search with secret agents, looking out for every clue
in smelly underground sewers, watching out for all the poo!

You'll be itching to find
those crafty creatures in the wood,
trying to hide among the animals
in any way they could.

You'll wish you knew why
whales and narwhals go by.
Swimming softly in moonlight
across the silky night sky.

You'll learn about the troop
of Arctic ninjas in the snow,
fighting giant icy spiders
using moves that they all know.

You'll imagine mighty monsters
turn your whole house upside down!
Would it make you laugh and smile
or would it make you frown?

Now you've found
all of these stories,
you'll wonder how they end.
Well, that's the most
exciting part.
It's down to you
my friend!

These stories are
yours to talk about,
draw or even write.
So, fire up your imagination.
You're in for a ride.
Hold tight!

OWLET PRESS

Growing into wisdom

Discover even more stories to treasure!

The next time you look up at the night sky, you might see the sparkling metal planet with all its robots and their robo-babies. A story about all the ways babies arrive into their families like IVF, surrogacy, donors and adoption.

RRP: £7.99

In the 'Polka Dot Pet Shop', where every animal is magical and marvellous, we find a plain, brown mouse who struggles to see how he fits in. Young readers learn about confidence, as the mouse realises his own unique talents.

RRP: £7.99

All the weasels in Westburrow Wood like to be the same, but not Wesley; he's obsessed with clothes! This story of acceptance helps children build empathy, by exploring themes around differences and identity.

RRP: £7.99

Follow @owletpress on social media or visit www.owletpress.com to learn more about us.